For my mother and father—*love, love, love!*

BEACH LANE BOOKS • An imprint of Simon & Schuster Children's Publishing Division • 1230 Avenue of the Americas, New York, New York 10020 • Copyright © 2012 by Keith Baker • All rights reserved, including the right of reproduction in whole or in part in any form. • BEACH LANE BOOKS is a trademark of Simon & Schuster, Inc. • For information about special discounts for bulk purchases, please contact Simon & Schuster Special Sales at 1-866-506-1949 or business@simonandschuster. com. • The Simon & Schuster Speakers Bureau can bring authors to your live event. For more information or to book an event, contact the Simon & Schuster Speakers Bureau at 1-866-248-3049 or visit our website at www.simonspeakers.com. • Book design by Sonia Chaghatzbanian • The text for this book is set in Frankfurter Medium. • The illustrations for this book are rendered digitally. • Manufactured in China • 1017 SCP • 10 9 8 7 • • Library of Congress Cataloging-in-Publication Data • Baker, Keith, 1953– • 1-2-3 peas / Keith Baker. —1st ed. • p. cm. • One two three peas • 123 peas • Summary: Busy little peas engage in their favorite activities as they introduce the numbers from one to 100. • ISBN 978-1-4424-4551-2 (hardcover) • ISBN 978-1-4424-6575-6 (eBook) • [1. Stories in rhyme. 2. Peas—Fiction. 3. Counting.] I. Title. II. Title: One two three peas. III. Title: 123 peas. • PZ8.3.B175Aah 2012 • [E]—dc23 • 2011034724

Keith Baker

1-2-3 peas

Beach Lane Books New York London Toronto Sydney New Delhi

1

ONE

pea searching—
look, look, look,

TWO

peas fishing—
hook, hook, hook.

2

3

THREE

peas boating—
row, row, row,

FOUR

peas planting—
grow, grow, grow.

FIVE

peas painting—
brush, brush, brush,

SIX peas traveling—
rush, rush, rush.

S E V E N

peas jumping—
splash, splash, splash!

7

EIGHT

peas racing—*dash, dash, dash.*

peas dancing—*round, round, round,*

TEN

peas building—
pound, pound, pound.

Eleven to nineteen—*skip, skip, skip!*

peas cutting—*snip, snip, snip.*

THIRTY

peas honking—
beep, beep, beep!

PEA-WEE TRUCKING

FORTY

peas napping—
sleep, sleep, sleep.

SIXTY

peas watching—*wow, wow, wow!*

SEVENTY

peas singing— *la, la, la,*

EIGHTY peas laughing—ha, ha, ha!

NINETY

peas floating—*free, free, free,*

HUNDRED

peas counting, *hap-pea as can be....*

Please count again with us!

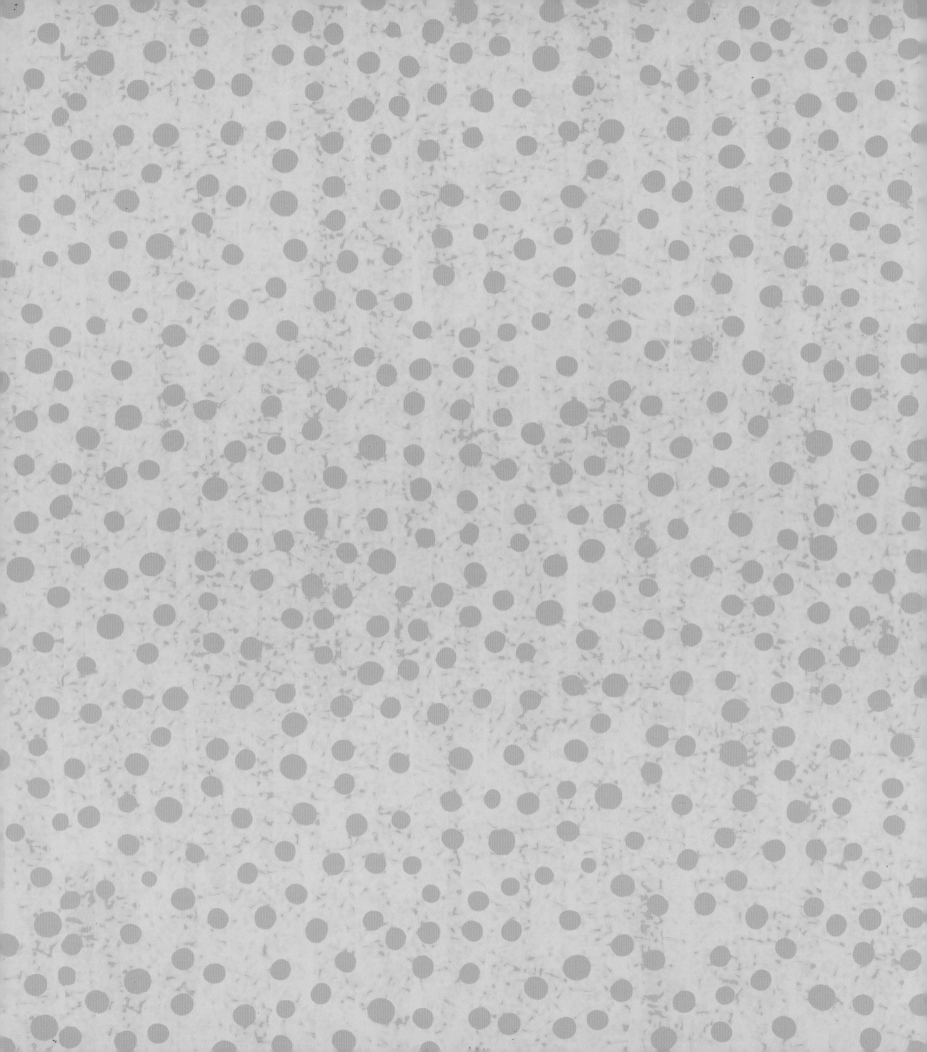